THE ALIEN APOCALYPSE

WHERE DO THEY COME FROM? AND WHY ARE THEY HERE?

FRANK MORIN

Library of Congress Control Number: 2020911701
ISBN 978-1-956010-08-4 (paperback)
ISBN 978-1-956010-11-4 (digital)

Copyright © 2021 by Frank Morin

All rights reserved. No part of this publication may be reproduced, distributed, or transmitted in any form or by any means, including photocopying, recording, or other electronic or mechanical methods without the prior written permission of the publisher. For permission requests, solicit the publisher via the address below.

Rushmore Press LLC
1 800 460 9188
www.rushmorepress.com

Printed in the United States of America

CONTENTS

Preface vii
Chapter 1 GODs Aliens Extraterrestrials 1
Chapter 2 The creation of humans The creation of
   Hybrid Celestial Entities 11
Chapter 3 Extraterrestrials and the craft they use... 21
Chapter 4 Relocating to the Moon 29
Chapter 5 Human's space progress
   Extraterrestrials in our skies 37
Chapter 6 Extraterrestrials attempts to
   communicate..45
Chapter 7 Unidentified Flying Objects "UFOs" 57
Chapter 8 Some after thoughts to topics
   discussed earlier...67

I dedicate this book to my son Thomas, whose encouragement and continuous checking on how I was progressing on the book, motivated me to complete the book. All my love – Dad.

PREFACE

Gods — Aliens — Extraterrestrials — we are intrigued by them — yet we are afraid of them, then there are people that don't believe they exist.

My book explains who the Extraterrestrials are and who are the Aliens and where they come from.

Most people believe Aliens and Extraterrestrials are the same Entities – they are NOT.

I start by explaining certain believe.

I also discuss other topics and after thoughts – mine and other peoples.

I also discuss Animal Mutilations – why they are happening – a lot of people will be surprised.

CHAPTER 1

GODS ALIENS EXTRATERRESTRIALS

Three topic's humans have been captivated with in an effort to provide an understanding for the meaning of these three words – topics.

All humans have conceived their own interpretations for these three topics. Some will favor one meaning or interpretations.

I'll begin with the topic "Gods" humans use this word so easily but have a difficult time believing in the true concept of God or his creative ability and supreme power.

God help you! May God be with you! God forgive you! God bless you! The gods! and words to this effect are used so easily and yet some of the people that use these phrases have trouble believing in God.

GOD – either we believe in God or we don't. If we believe – do we believe in one God or in the many human conceived gods? Some humans believe in God with conditions.

God – the word humans use without a real understanding of the actual and true meaning or of God's true potential.

Humans' almost always want to minimize God's power, ability and knowledge because they are not capable of comprehending these supernatural attributes with their limited minds. Some humans preconceived opinion of God is that "God" is only superior to the humanly definition.

Humanly as defined in the dictionary – in a human manner, within human ability or knowledge, from a human viewpoint.

Humans understanding and concept of the power of a Supreme Being is very limited and difficult for them to comprehend. Humans instinctually tend to label any "ENTITY" with a higher intellect as a god, an Alien or an Extraterrestrial. God the Father is the Supreme Entity with an unlimited ability, knowledge and power.

Aliens do not come from the planet earth that is why they are Aliens. Extraterrestrials come from the planet earth and that is why they are NOT Aliens. Also Extraterrestrials and Aliens are definitely NOT gods as some humans would want us to believe.

Humans are now also extraterrestrials. I'll explain this and the previous statements later.

Let me get back to the topic of God.

In monotheistic religions "GOD" the Supreme Entity is the creator and ruler of the universe.

God create the Universe, Celestial Entities (Angels), the planet Earth, Humanoids, Humans, all the plants and other creatures that were put on the planet Earth.

God created the universe to demonstrate to us humans his creative powers and the immense creation he controls.

God instilled a lot of information on earth, from the largest creatures to the smallest one cell organism. God also placed a lot of information in the universe he created.

Who is "GOD" and why does the bible state, "let US make man in OUR image, in OUR likeness" Gen. 1: 26. The use of the words "US and OUR" refers to the Holy Trinity. The Holy Trinity is God the Father, the creator of everything, God the Son, who will judge all humans that were created in the "image and likeness" and God the Holy Spirit, who provides a soul for all humans that God the Son will judge.

God the Son "Jesus Christ" was born a human for two reasons: one was to die for our sins and the second was to witness and experience all the emotions and temptations humans are exposed to. This knowledge will provide him the actual experience so that he will judge humans fairly and just.

Jesus called himself "the Son of Man" this showed that he had the authority and power of a divine person, and yet also was a man. Jesus was transfigured from a man to a God.

What does God look like?

There is only one description of God the Father and that is the description presented in the bible.

Again, depending on what you believe will also describe the appearance of the entity you call a god.

Believers in the bible can only use the description presented in the bible for the appearance of God the Father.

The bible states; Ezekiel 1: 27-28

"A figure like that of a man, I saw that from what appeared to be his waist up he looked like glowing metal, as if full of fire, and that from there down he looked like fire; and brilliant light surrounded him. Like the appearance of a rainbow in the clouds on a rainy day, so was the radiance around him". This is the appearance of the likeness of the glory of the Lord – God the Father.

God the Father has presented himself to humans in various forms and that is what I believe confuses humans about Gods appearance.

Humans have always attempted and want to portray the appearance of God the Son "Jesus Christ" according to their demographics.

I believe Jesus Christ left his image on the cloth of Turin so that we would have no doubt of his appearance.

Humans know Jesus was born in the Jewish faith and his appearance should reflect the Jewish appearance left on the cloth of Turin. God the Holy Spirit we believe because of our faith.

Nonbelievers in the bible describe their gods as looking like, any various beings or Idols formed or developed in their minds. Their gods possess intelligence or abilities greater than humans and in some areas of this world their gods are preconceive with a divine status.

That is why humans considered Aliens, gods in antiquity, in the present day some individuals call Extraterrestrials – the gods or Aliens.

These individuals are probably confused and don't realize that only God the Father has Supreme powers.

Humans not being able to recognize the difference between an act performed by an "Entity" of higher intelligence and an act performed by the "Supreme Entity" tend to attribute anything above their understanding as godly.

In Antiquity humans explained events and technology that they could not understand as acts or events that were caused or performed by the gods they conceived.

The Egyptians had the Sun god and also a lot of other gods.

One Egyptian pharaoh even tried to present the concept that there was only one God. Egyptians didn't want to believe that then and some humans don't want to believe that now.

The Greeks had their own stories and myths about Zeus and other gods. The Greeks stories told how Zeus procreated with human woman. I believe this was the

Greeks version for the interpretation of the story told in the bible. Gen. 6: 4

The Romans had the god Jupiter and other gods.

Humans in different locations on earth have also conceived their own forms of gods and some of these gods were given a divine status by the humans.

These human conceived gods served whatever purpose the humans wanted them to serve.

This mythical form of thinking played right into the abilities of the Celestial Entities or as humans call them "Angels" and the Hybrid Celestial children's prodding for these Angels to perform the roles of these different gods.

The Celestial Entities "Angels" demonstrated their superior intelligence and technological capabilities by accepting and playing the roles of these human conceived gods for the amazement of all the Egyptians, Greeks, Romans and other humans.

The entities that provided the advance knowledge in different locations on earth were described as different in appearance as to the population of those locations.

The bible states; "they were the heroes of old, men of renown". Gen. 6: 4

In antiquity humans would always give the credit to their conceive gods for events and technology they did not understand.

In the present day, events and technology that humans don't understand, humans give the credit to Extraterrestrials, who some of these individuals also call them, the gods.

These Extraterrestrial have only existed about twenty thousand years, when they were born.

They have been flying in their superior craft for about eighteen thousand years.

For definition purpose – let's put names to different Entities.

God the Father– Supreme Entity

Celestial Entities – Angels – Aliens and other titles

Children of Angeles and human woman – Nephilim – Hybrid Celestial entities - extraterrestrials

Man and Woman – Hybrid Human beings – Humans

Other titles of Celestial Entities;

In the beginning God created Celestial Entities and they are called – Angels, sons of God, Gods messengers, protectors of humans, and protectors of the sky, Anakites, Aliens and Extraterrestrials.

Celestial Entities "Angels" are capable of possessing physical bodies or nonphysical bodies.

One example of Angels possessing physical bodies can be found in Gen. 19: 1-3 in the Holy Bible NIV "Angels washed their feet and ate a meal".

There are many examples of Angels possessing physical or nonphysical bodies and later I will point out some more examples.

Aliens — Who are they?

I need to clarify one issue: We have to be careful NOT to confuse "An Alien" with "An Extraterrestrial entity" even though humans tend to consider them to be the same entity.

Alien – the dictionary states – foreign, different in nature.

Extraterrestrial – the dictionary states – from outside the earth atmosphere, I believe it should also state any entity that has traveled somewhere else from earth.

There are two types of entities that humans call "Aliens" Angels and Hybrid Celestial children "Nephilims" as they are called in the bible.

These two types of entities possess a higher level of intelligence but the technology comes from the Celestial Entities "Angels" and they use these attributes to impress us humans with a lasting effect.

ANGEL's are truly the real and only Aliens in the whole universe; they are not gods and yet they are foreign, they come from heaven, somewhere other than earth.

Angels are different in nature. They can possess physical or nonphysical bodies.

Angels do NOT require any form of a craft to travel. When Angels use their physical bodies on earth, they are called Anakites.

Sometimes, Angeles are mistaken for Extraterrestrials because they are in the same craft with their Hybrid Celestial children (Nephilims) and they are using a physical body that makes them appear to look almost human.

The Extraterrestrials we observe have physical bodies and they DO require a craft (Unidentified Flying Object – UFO) for transportation.

These Extraterrestrials are Hybrid Celestial entities and they require some type of craft to travel because they are the children of Angels and human woman and they have human form bodies like their mothers.

Angeles on the other hand are Celestial Entities and since they possess the ability of having physical bodies (allowing them to procreate, eat meals) or nonphysical bodies – such as when they were observed traveling in space without a craft.

Why do we call them Alien's or Extraterrestrials?

Human's call them alien's because humans want to fantasize that the entities they call Extraterrestrials or

Aliens have traveled here millions of miles from other planets or galaxies.

Humans also consider them strange – different looking – because they are using the descriptions of Extraterrestrials that were buried, recovered or the Extraterrestrials seen by people that have been abducted.

Humans have a difficult time accepting Angels as being real because, 1. They have never seen an Angel or 2. It would mean that they believe in God or 3. Their entire make believe fantasizes would go up in smoke.

Humans that have been abducted and have asked the abductors where they were from have been told by the Extraterrestrials that they come from the Orion star cluster.

Those extraterrestrials were probably Angels, and "they" probably do come from the Orion star cluster which is 1500 light years from earth.

Of course Angels that are in the UFOs using their physical bodies are going to tell you the truth – which is – that they come from the Orion star cluster. Angels are capable of traveling 1500 light years in their non-physical bodies.

I will discuss Extraterrestrials in more detail later in the book after I explain their existence.

CHAPTER 2

THE CREATION OF HUMANS THE CREATION OF HYBRID CELESTIAL ENTITIES

The big bang theory, described by scientist as the source of creating the Universe, cannot be explained in human methodology. That is because the universe was created so that it could "not" be explained by human scientist or in any humanly explanation.

According to scientist the Universe was created about 13 billion years ago. Earth, the perfect planet/world was created 4 and half billion years ago with all its potential and the protection capabilities that God installed, for us humans.

We humans can not appreciate this beautiful and perfect planet so we abuse it and take it for granted. Everything on this planet was put here for a purpose not just by chance.

Humans fanaticize how they will travel to other planets and galaxies. How they will conquer space travel and perform all the fantasies portrayed in the movies.

The truth is the Entities – we call them Extraterrestrials – have already traveled to other planets and have the actual experience of space travel.

They will enlighten us humans to the dangers and true possibilities of space travel and travel to other planets.

We humans know a little about traveling in space, we traveled to the moon and back.

I believe scientist want and expect everything to be explained by our laws of physics. The human's laws of physics do not apply to Extraterrestrials – their craft can make 90degree turns and stop in midair – and I am certain that the human laws of physics do not apply to God, the Supreme creator.

Let us take something we can relate to, what would it take to "CREATE" a Human being?

Let us start with the obvious parts – the head, contained within the head is the largest most complicated computer, the brain.

Also contained in the head is the eyes, ears, nose, mouth and a lot of special function organs that we take for granted, all enclosed in the skin which, besides providing protection also contain more special functions and hair.

All these parts are very complicated, but we can't forget the muscles, nerves, blood vessels, lymph nodes and the skull, which contain the teeth. Again all these also contain special function capabilities.

This is only the head, now we will talk about the body. The body – we have the Skeleton, the lungs, the heart, the stomach, the liver, the kidneys, the spleen, the pancreas, the gallbladder, the small and large intestines, the muscles, nerves, blood vessels, lymph nodes and fat for the arms, legs, chest, stomach, male and female body parts. Again all these parts contain special functions capabilities.

The bible states; Gen. 2:7

"God formed the man from the dust of the ground".

Can we humans comprehend this creative process?

Turning the dust of the ground into all the parts mentioned above and forming a male and female, I don't think we can.

Scientist attempt to explain creation, but they can only explain creation in a humanly experience concept "evolution" or as some scientist say, everything just came together by chance.

I can NOT believe anything on this planet or in the whole universe came about by chance.

There are too many factors that would keep chance from forming even a simple one-cell creature.

God's first creation of humans "in his own image and likeness" was over 50 thousand years ago. The reason for this inference is because we can only piece together their human existence from the evidence they left behind.

The Cro-Magnon cave drawings and their fossils provide us with an insight to their existence. Experts have spent a great amount of effort and time performing this verification task.

The bible states; Gen. 1: 27-28

"So God created man in his own image, in the image of God he create him; male and female he created them". God blessed them and said to them, "be fruitful and increase in number, fill the earth and subdue it".

The rest of this story and the lives of this male and female and their descendents was not documented. The whole story and the lives of Adam and Eve and their descendents is completely documented in the bible.

I believe the explanation for this is that the descendents of the first male and female were not to become the linage of Jesus Christ but they were to populate the earth and provide mates for a lot of the descendents of Adam and Eve.

The human lineage for Jesus Christ was from Adam and Eve. That is why the bible tracks all descendents of Adam and Eve in the lineage of Jesus Christ until his birth and then that lineage ends.

Humanoids were present on earth before 50 thousand years but they were not created "in the image and likeness of God".

They were the Neanderthal humanoids and they were present on earth about 150 thousand years ago.

Anthropology has verified that there was two distinctive types' of humans – Neanderthal humanoids – and – Cro-Magnon humans – were both present in the fifty thousand years' time period in human's history.

I believe that Cro-Magnon humans were God's creation in his image and likeness and that is why the Neanderthal humanoids went extinct – maybe – maybe not.

Neanderthal humanoids were and are survivors and this group has survived over a hundred and fifty thousand years. Their development did not advance beyond the level of hunter-gather in that whole time period.

I believe Neanderthal humanoids could be the creatures that we are calling Big Foot or all the other names we have given that type of humanoid.

Neanderthal humanoids are the true caveman. They left the cave drawings and artifacts that Cro-Magnon humans who were created about 50 thousand years ago continued to use and improve.

I believe there are two other main differences besides appearance between Neanderthal humanoids and Cro-Magnon humans.

Cro-Magnon humans have the ability to verbally communicate with each other and they have a higher level of intelligence.

Let us assume that Big Foot is a descendent of the Neanderthal humanoids. All the information I have heard or read about mentions that Big Foot makes animal sounds to communicate. I don't believe they can communicate verbally.

Evolutionists believe humans evolved from a single cell to the Ape and then through all the levels of evolution to the present day human.

I believe Atheists or non-believers in God have to present a different source for their creation and their evolution since they don't want to believe that God created all humans.

We humans are hybrids – a mixture of Neanderthal woman and the two creations of Cro-Magnon humans.

I believe the statement in the bible "in the image and likeness of God" means that God had an image of humans. Humans should be creative, intelligent and able to communicate verbally plus we should have a more human appearance – not an ape like Neanderthal appearance.

God's second creation of a male "in his image and likeness" was about 20 thousand years ago. The creation of Adam and then of Eve is well documented in the bible. Gen. 2: 21-22

Some people want to believe that the first man created in Gods image and likeness and Adam are the same man.

I believe God started with a new man, and a completely different woman.

The reason I emphasis that Eve was a completely different woman is because she was not created from the dust of the ground.

The bible states; "God formed the man from the dust of the ground and breathed into his nostrils the breath of life and the man became a living being". Gen. 2: 7

The bible also states; Gen. 2: 21-22 "God caused the man to fall into a deep sleep; and while he was sleeping, he took one of the man's ribs and closed up the place with flesh. Then God made a woman from the rib he had taken out of the man, and he brought her to the man".

A proposition could be drawn from the previous two statements concerning the color of the skin of the man and the woman in the first creation and Adam in the second creation.

All three are created from the dust of the earth, which I believe would produce a light brown skin colored Entity.

The creation of the woman Eve was from Adams "white" rib.

I believe that would produce what we humans would call a "white" woman.

We add to this white woman "blonde hair" and "blue eyes" – I believe that would portray what humans and apparently Celestial Entities "Angels" would consider a beautiful woman.

After the creation of Adam and Eve, the bible states; Gen. 6: 1-3 "When man began to increase in number on the earth and daughters were born to them, the sons of God saw that the daughters of men were beautiful, and they married any of them they chose".

I believe this is where the blonde hair and blue eyes were introduced in humans.

Then the different shades of eye color came from the mixture of blue and brown eyes.

I believe Neanderthal humanoids came from Africa and since Cro-Magnon humans are mixed with Neanderthal woman, I believe that is why scientist concluded all humans come from Africa.

Scientist cannot explain how blonde hair and blue eyes developed from the humanoids of Africa.

I believe the different blood types in humans can be traced to the Neanderthal woman, the Cro-Magnon man and woman of the first creation and Adam and Eve of the second creation. I believe the Neanderthal woman passed on the trait of a semi hairy body through interbreeding.

Interbreeding caused the different shades of skin color and hairy bodies. The light brown skin color of the first Cro-Magnon male and female and Adam mixed with the white skin color of Eve caused lighter shades.

Humans caused darker shades of skin color through color selection.

White humans consider themselves superior to all other shades of humans. I will provide evidence later that this is not true.

What does all this have to do with Aliens?

As always you have to start in the beginning of any story and then you proceed with the rest of the story.

That is the beginning of this story, so now I will get to the part of explaining about Extraterrestrials.

I will be presenting some views and conceptions that might be hard to accept or agree with.

CHAPTER 3
EXTRATERRESTRIALS AND THE CRAFT THEY USE

The craft (UFO's) used by Hybrid Celestial entities " Extraterrestrials" if examined closely, require or have "windows", ramps "doors" and are built with materials that are earthly but superior in manufacturing.

A UFO hunter team located a piece of metal from a craft "UFO" that had crashed in New Mexico.

The metal was analyzed in a well-recognized lab and the results found was the piece of metal contained earthly elements and one element that could not be identified, which I attribute to "superior manufacturing".

Hybrid Celestial children cannot travel like their fathers "Angels"; they have to travel by the use of a craft (UFO).

Hybrid Celestial children's intelligence is superior to human intelligence, but their physical bodies, I believe have almost the same limitations as humans.

Humans can only perceive a higher intelligence entity as an Alien or an Extraterrestrial. Someone that they fantasize has traveled here from a distant planet or galaxy or a god.

Angels being a Celestial Entity have no limitations when they travel using their nonphysical bodies and they have no boundaries of where they travel in the universe. In this view, the fantasy of an Alien traveling here from a distant planet or galaxy is correct since Angels are Aliens.

Celestial entities "Angels" intelligence is greatly superior to both the Hybrid Celestial children and especially Hybrid humans (Man).

The Hybrid Celestial children travel in space and around the earth using the craft (UFO's) produced by (Angels) their fathers and them.

Angels have always been aware of the vastness and the possibilities in the universe. They have traveled the vastness and explored the planets in various star clusters.

They know what star clusters had planets – not like earth, but planets that would be capable of supporting life if used in a certain way.

After the creation of Adam and Eve, the bible states; Gen. 6: 1-3 "when man began to increase in number on the earth and daughters were born to them, the sons of

God saw that the daughters of men were beautiful, and they married any of them they chose".

Then the Lord said, "My spirit will not contend with man forever, for he is mortal his days will be a hundred and twenty years".

Adam and Eve and their descendents lived over 900 years in the beginning. Adam lived 930 years, and then he died.

After the time of the flood mentioned in the bible, Adam's and Eve's descendents started to live fewer years, now we do good if a few humans live over 100 years.

I heard that the meaning of the word "Nephilim" is supposed to be "men that came down from above".

I submit that the meaning of the word Nephilim is "Hybrid Celestial Entities".

The bible states without the bracketed words; Gen. 6: 4 "the Nephilim [Hybrid Celestial Entities] were on the earth in those days – and afterward – when the sons of God [Angels] went to the daughters of men and had children by them. They were the hero's of old, men of renown".

The Nephilim – the Hybrid Celestial Entities – "the children of Angels and human woman" were definitely on earth in those days and afterwards. Hybrid Celestial entities had good and bad traits. They knew good and evil, Gen. 3: 22 they are part human.

In the days of the Greek, the stories and myths "of the hero's of old, men of renown" was only a humanly way of explaining the technology and performance of the Angels and their Hybrid children, which we humans called "Gods" then and "Aliens" or "Extraterrestrials" in the present.

Humans are more willing to accept the stories and myths about the Greeks god Zeus procreating with human woman, yet we question and some people can't accept that Angels could procreate.

The Hybrid Celestial children have been on earth less than twenty thousand years and very well fit the description of the Egyptian, Greek and Roman gods and other human conceived gods in past time and Extraterrestrials now.

All the stories and myths in antiquity were really about the Angels and the Hybrid Celestial children using their higher intelligence and advance technology to produce the amazing effects stated in the myths and stories.

Hybrid Celestial children having human tendencies could and did corrupt science and produced repulsive and offensive creatures. This substantiates the stories and myths told by, the Egyptians, Greeks, Romans and others.

God created man and I believe to understand humans better God walked with Enoch, the bible states; Gen. 5: 22-24

"And after he became the father of Methuselah, Enoch walked with God 300 years and had other sons and daughters. Altogether, Enoch lived 365 years.

Enoch walked with God; then he was no more, because God took him away".

Less than twenty thousand years ago Angels, their Hybrid Celestial children and their mothers formed communities.

These communities used the superior intelligence and advance technology of the Angels.

The bible states – Hear, O Israel. You are now about to cross the Jordan to go in and dispossess nations greater and stronger than you, with large cities that have walls up to the sky. The people are strong and tall – Anakites! You know about them and have heard it said: "who can stand up against the Anakites?" Deuteronomy 9: 1-2

About eighteen thousand years ago – when Angels became aware that, God was planning to destroy the humans on earth with a flood, the Angels decided to move their communities off the planet earth. Angels started to make preparations so that their Hybrid Celestial children and their mothers would be able to travel in space.

Angels realize that their Hybrid Celestial children and their mothers would require all craft to be airtight or space suits would have to be worn during transportation since their ability to travel in space was restricted.

Angels with their superior intelligence produced devices and some were shared with humans – the Egyptian light bulb – they realized they could allow humans to use the devices but had to control the exposure, since the technology was beyond humans understanding.

Angels produced different types of craft, large craft for transporting building materials and smaller but quicker craft for transporting individuals.

In Puma Punku, Bolivia stone structures were discovered that humans are unable to agree as to the reason for their existence. The stones are very advance in design and production techniques.

I believe logic dictates that the stone structures half built in Puma Punku, Bolivia were not planned as complete buildings. This was where the Angels and their Hybrid sons practiced the building techniques that would be used when building permanent facilities on the moon.

Bolivia also provided the Granite and Diorite stones used for constructing the airtight structures on the moon.

These types of stones would last a long time.

The craft used to transport and relocate their Hybrid communities to the dark side of the moon were also used as temporary living quarters while the permanent facilities were being built before and after the flood on earth.

The Angels and their Hybrid sons built permanent facilities in the moon using solid Granite and utilizing the techniques practiced in Puma Punku, Bolivia. Solid Granite will last for thousands of years where as any other type of building material would not last as long.

I also believe a reasonable explanation for where the top of the mountains in Peru, that individuals have stated are missing, is that they were consumed.

The consumption of the top of the mountains in Peru, where the Nazca lines exist, were removed and used by the Angels and their Hybrid sons to obtain the vast amounts of various minerals they needed.

The (Gold, Silver, Copper, Aluminum, Iron and whatever other minerals they needed) were used in the production of their different craft and other essential needs for the construction and every day operation of their community's.

CHAPTER 4
RELOCATING TO THE MOON

As stated earlier when the Angels found out that God was planning to destroy the humans on earth with a flood. They decided that they would move the Hybrid communities to the back or the dark side of the moon.

Why relocate to the back or dark side of the moon?

Because the moon was close to earth.

The closeness of the moon to earth provided the Hybrid Celestial community with the supplies that was needed and could not be produced or obtained anywhere else.

The facilities built on the moon were permanent and completely – airtight – what humans would consider a moon station. These facilities still exist on the moon.

The relocation of the Hybrid communities to the moon was a learning experience for the Angels "fathers" on space travel and providing for their Hybrid Celestial children and their human mothers.

Angels never had to deal with the challenges of providing different types of food, their storage, cooking supplies, the disposal of waste, the production of breathable air, the transportation of water and its storage, light utilizing light bulbs, and all other human requirements the Hybrid communities needed.

Later, Angels and their Hybrid sons produced craft that could be used for transportation and as a habitat. The present day Unidentified Flying Objects "UFO's".

On earth all the Hybrid community special requirements were provided, on the moon in the closed environment that the Hybrid communities had to live in, everything had to be provided artificially or supplied from earth by the Angels.

After the Angels relocated their communities to the moon, the first Extraterrestrials, they would travel back and forth from the moon to earth both for information and supplies.

This is the start of Extraterrestrial travel and the first use of a craft to travel off the planet earth.

The Hybrid Celestial children and their mothers were the first Extraterrestrials and they colonized the moon.

When the children grew older, they wanted to try different technologies and conquer space travel – sound familiar.

When the Angels realize, the flood on earth was over, they started the process of relocating some of their community's back on earth.

The communities were glad to be back on earth, but they had become accustomed to living in a smaller controlled environment.

Angels and their Hybrid sons built colonies on earth where they could utilize their advanced knowledge and technology – Deuteronomy 9: 1-2

They relocated to areas where humans had not yet developed or where humans were in a primitive state of development.

They also realized that their craft were capable of venturing to the bottom of the ocean and could remain there as long as they desired.

In less than eighteen thousand years Angels and their Hybrid sons have developed craft with the ability to maintain a whole community. These craft could stay at the bottom of our oceans, fly in our skies and even fly in space around and to our moon.

Angels and their hybrid sons developed spacecraft science and created transportation that would allow them to travel to Mars. Some of the Hybrid community traveled to Mars and developed a colony there, which was abandoned.

The same as humans, the Hybrid children saw Mars as a place to colonize. They attempted to colonize Mars and maybe we will locate some of the artifacts or the bacteria left by the Hybrid colonization, if we are lucky.

Space travel was exciting, but Hybrid Celestial children like their mothers had limitations. Again the same as us humans, the Hybrid Celestial children wanted to travel to the other stars and planets.

One advantage they had was their fathers were Celestial beings and they possessed superior intelligence and the experience of space travel.

Celestial beings possessed the technological knowledge to get their Hybrid Celestial children to the star cluster Sirius, which is eight light years from earth.

Only the Hybrid Celestial children traveled to the star cluster Sirius where they developed a community.

The community developed in the star cluster Sirius is maintained by Hybrid Celestial children only.

Their fathers – the Angels – would travel there by their own means, using their nonphysical bodies. Probably half the fathers would stay there and then they would rotate.

Hybrid Celestial children's limitations are a result of the half human bodies they possess, their bodies were being used for exposures other than their intended purpose.

Another condition that Hybrid children were exposed to was space radiation. Space travel to Mars was in weeks.

Angels realized that for their Hybrid children to travel in space – especially long distances – a different mode of travel had to be utilized. Angels observed the effects of space radiation on their Hybrid children – the skin was destroyed faster than it could reproduce – so they started to use Vortex travel.

Since Angels had traveled the universe, they wanted to share the beauty and experience, of space travel.

Vortex travel is an excellent means of transferring items from one location to another, but Vortex travel has certain side effects on the human body. Travel to the star cluster Sirius by Hybrid Celestial children was through Vortex travel.

Extraterrestrial's where do they come from?

They come from earth. Humans are now also Extraterrestrial's because we traveled to the moon, but where have Hybrid Celestial children traveled?

Hybrid Celestial children have traveled to the Moon, Mars and the Sirius star cluster. The beginning of space travel by Extraterrestrials in spacecraft was before the flood.

A lot of humans fantasize about Extraterrestrials traveling to earth from a faraway planet or another galaxy, in make believe and exorbitant spaceships.

Humans also fantasize Extraterrestrials with weird or scary appearance. In bodies that have been created by movie makers and people's imaginations.

I believe once we communicate with Extraterrestrials we will be presented with the knowledge that Extraterrestrials are Hybrid Celestial Entities – Nephilims – from earth.

Maybe, what we see as Extraterrestrials entity's bodies – or the description of their appearance is only a synthetic covering that is used to cover up the effects of years of space travel and radiation on Hybrid Celestial Entities.

These are the Extraterrestrials that humans call "the Grays" because of the color of their skin. These are the older generation of Hybrid Celestial Entities.

The colony on Mars was abandoned and mostly removed. This was due to the distance from earth and the difficulty of supplying food and water.

Humans fantasize about traveling to Mars and producing all the food they would require to support a small colony for a certain period of time but the reality is, that was attempted before and it did not work.

Space radiation was the convincing factor that prompted the abandonment of the colony on Mars.

We are accustomed and take for granted all the protections provided for us on earth, which are not provided on Mars.

In the star cluster Sirius, Angels located a planet that didn't have an atmosphere, but was covered with water.

The Angels explained to their Hybrid children that, if they traveled there, and colonized the planet, they would have to live underwater to avoid space radiation.

The Hybrid Celestial children that colonized the planet in the Sirius star cluster obtained their supplies via the Vortex system.

They obtained metals, oil, coal, wood and whatever else is transported from earth through the Vortex system.

As I stated before the colony on the dark side or backside of the moon is still maintained and operational.

This was demonstrated when Extraterrestrial craft and Celestial Entity's started observing our spacecraft and the Russians spacecraft on their trips to space and America's eventually landing on the moon.

NASA has had astronauts actually transmit statements that they were being tracked or observed by unknown craft.

The Russian astronaut's also transmitted communications with their ground control that they were seeing Angels or Celestial Entities outside their spacecraft.

The Angels were traveling in space without any type of craft and only using their nonphysical bodies – amazing.

We humans cannot comprehend the abilities of Angels, but apparently their abilities allow them to perform feats that we would consider impossible.

CHAPTER 5

HUMAN'S SPACE PROGRESS EXTRATERRESTRIALS IN OUR SKIES

I believe our spacecraft are being observed and monitored by Extraterrestrials and Celestial Entities.

American and Russian astronauts have observed and recorded various incidents in space that verify that they were being watched and monitored so that no accident in space was causing a human life. Maybe someday the American Government will allow the astronauts to discuss these incidents.

During America's last lunar landing, after the astronauts landed on the moon, they used the lunar land rover to explore the backside of the moon. They didn't explore the backside of the moon very long.

I believe they saw or were confronted by the Hybrid Celestial children "Extraterrestrials" from the colony on the backside of the moon.

The astronauts returned to the lunar landing craft in what appeared to be a panic state. They immediately contacted ground control on the secret frequencies and none of the communication was transmitted over the air.

If we could have listened to the communication between the astronauts and ground control some very interesting facts could have been discovered, pertaining to what they saw or who they saw.

The astronauts not only discovered the colony, but they must have been instructed not to return to the moon, because NO MORE lunar landings have occurred since then, over forty years and not a single attempt has been made to return to the moon.

America and the other countries then switched priorities from exploring the moon to building a space station.

This was to provide the American people and the people of the other countries with a purpose for the expenditures of time, money and materials.

The American people should look back in time and remember the closed environment experiment that was proposed, build and failed here on earth.

If we humans can't succeed with a closed self-contained environment project here on earth, why are we so arrogant or stupid to think we can succeed in space?

The space station would have only accommodated a small number of personnel "I wonder who they would be" and it would have to be close enough to earth to resupply.

I believe that our Government and the other Governments were building the space station as a refuge for a small group of selected individuals.

The 2012 prophecy caused a lot of panic in the world.

I started working on this book years before the 2012 prophecy became popular. I am convinced that the space station was a rush up project due to the 2012 prophecy.

The doom's day preppers were building different kinds of living quarters for their survival after December 21, 2012.

Now that the 2012 prophecy has passed, the space station project has lost its importance and now the American government and the other country's governments have moved on to other projects.

The earth has kept us humans busy, throughout the world with earthquakes, tidal waves, hurricanes and tornados.

The storms that devastated certain parts of the United States also kept Americans occupied.

All this did not threaten any governments only the common people. Governments have to continue and I believe that is the thinking of the people in government.

I wonder what a government would do without the people it is set up to govern and care for.

Let me get back to the subject of Extraterrestrials.

They are important because they possess a lot of information that we humans will find both useful and enlightening.

Extraterrestrials, are they flying in our skies – if they are – why?

Yes, Extraterrestrials are flying in our skies and in the skies of almost every country on this planet. Extraterrestrials are Hybrid Celestial children and they also consider earth their home. Extraterrestrials have been flying in our skies for about eighteen thousand years.

Looking back in human history we have the evidence, skeptics will attempt to down play the evidence, but I believe the evidence will and has proven the existence of Hybrid Celestial entities "Extraterrestrials" on earth.

The evidence that we acknowledge goes back only to antiquity – then we called the evidence myths or stories.

I believe the evidence goes back more than 17 thousand years. If we evaluate the evidence left behind we can make a better determination as to how far back it goes.

Extraterrestrials "Nephilims" have left evidence of their presence or existence all over this planet/world.

They have shared knowledge and technology with us humans at different times in our history and with different cultures in different parts of this world.

Extraterrestrials "Nephilims" realized that any evidence they wanted to leave as structures and to have them last through time. The structures had to be built from huge stones or the structures would be easy to destroy.

Evidence left behind and seen at different locations,

Puma Punku, Bolivia I believe is dated 14000 to 17000 years old.

Structures in southeastern Turkey, Stones with advance carvings are dated about 12000 B.C.

Jericho is dated to about 9000 B.C.

Monolith stones at Carnac, France dated to about 4500 years old.

Egypt's pyramids are 4000 to 5000 years old.

There is the Saqqara Egyptian artifact that appeared to resemble an aircraft, it was reproduced to scale, tested and it flew and landed dated – about 4000 to 5000 years old.

Machu Picchu, Peru, Stones molded into place is dated about 5000 years old.

Tiahuanaco, Bolivia – the wall of stone faces of all races – abandoned in 1100 AD.

I am not surprised that numerous sightings of UFO's were observed in 1200 AD. Ancient art with drawings of flying craft also do not surprise me.

I believe that if we knew what was going to happen in history and we were able to witness the event by flying to the event, I believe we would fly there and witness the event as the paintings demonstrate.

Objects that rose from the sea close to Columbus' ship – time in history 1400s.

UFO crashed in Aurora, Texas and an Extraterrestrial had a funeral and was buried in the cemetery – time in history 1897.

UFO crashed in Roswell NM – Extraterrestrial bodies were recovered – time in history 1947.

All this evidence is treated as the sighting of a UFO in the sky of Phoenix, Arizona. Make a joke of it or deny it and maybe it will be treated as not being true and forgotten.

The people that saw the UFO over Phoenix, Arizona on March 1997 didn't think the joke was funny. I understand that there are pranksters attempting to fool people but their foolish and childish attempts don't work.

If the evidence is not a prankster's attempt – then we should treat the evidence as real and true – in an attempt to accept and understand what is really happening.

I believe that people are honest and want to share their amazing experience with other individuals and the U.S. government, but they are confronted with negative and sometimes threatening actions. Who would want to share anything with someone that ridicules or threatens them or their family?

All the people that come forward and tell their story are brave and by sharing their stories they are spreading the truth and will be rewarded when they know the truth about Extraterrestrials.

I hope all the people that have an experience of sighting an Extraterrestrial craft realize that more and more people will be experiencing these sighting.

CHAPTER 6

EXTRATERRESTRIALS ATTEMPTS TO COMMUNICATE

Maybe the Extraterrestrials are trying to communicate and share information with us.

Humans have wondered are Extraterrestrials here to study humans or to procreate with us. I don't believe Nephilims have to study humans because they are half human.

I do believe they are trying to replace Extraterrestrials that were lost through accidents and spacecraft crashes.

We humans keep fantasizing, what would the experience be if we could communicate with Extraterrestrials.

How interesting it would be if we could reminisce with the Nephilims about our history and how and when they influenced it?

I believe that if we really want to communicate with the Extraterrestrials "Nephilims", first we have to believe in them.

Second we have to quit relying on the U.S. Government for information and approval.

Humans are a spice that is ingrained with the concept of show me the proof and then I'll believe it – maybe.

Extraterrestrials have the answers to most of our questions, but any time they try to communicate with us humans, they are met with physical threats.

Extraterrestrials attempted to communicate with the White House in the late 1940's and they were chased away by jets.

Again, Extraterrestrials attempted to communicate with the White House on April 27, 2005 and they were chased out of the air space over the White House.

I understand the apprehension of the personnel in the White House, but some protocol should be established to deal with such attempts and not endanger the President.

How many other attempts have been made by the Extraterrestrials to communicate, we will never know?

Nephilims are now attempting to communicate with us humans in a more non-threatening and intellectual level – hopefully – we will be able to decipher and understand their communication.

An example is the Bent Water England incident where active duty personnel witnessed a UFO landing. Jim, John, Bud and Lt. Col. Halt witnessed the UFO that landed in the Rendlesham forest. Lt. Col. Halt produced a tape recording of what he saw, heard and felt while observing the UFO craft.

When Jim Penniston touched the craft it transferred a message using Binary Code.

They attempted to document what happened and yet they were threatened and encouraged to forget the whole incident by U.S. agents.

The message: Exploration of humanity for planetary – the "CE" was added to the word advance to complete the word, as were the words "NUOUS" added to the word continuous.

I believe the message was an attempt by the Nephilims to explain their purpose for trying to communicate with us humans.

I believe the message was meant to say "Exploration of humanity for the planetary advancement continues". I hope the next time we receive a binary coded message, we receive a complete message.

Another means Nephilims are using to communicate with us is by the use of Crop Circles. I believe there is a meaning to their designs – probably mathematical.

Crop Circles have appeared at different locations with a variety of designs. I believe the designs are different because they have different meanings and just like a puzzle, some are easy and some are more difficult to decipher.

Humans have been misinformed and lead to believe that Extraterrestrials want to destroy, subdue or control us.

Humans are extremely violent spices and we conceive any attempt by Extraterrestrials to communicate as an aggressive act.

Extraterrestrials have been vilified to us humans with all the movies that portray Extraterrestrials as aggressive and dangerous creatures. Humans like to live in their make believe world.

Extraterrestrials possess technology that is extremely superior to human technology and if they wanted to be aggressive they would be capable of doing as they pleased.

They have demonstrated this ability on different occasions when they had to defend themselves.

Extraterrestrial craft (UFO's) are able to appear and disappear, travel at amazing speeds and pretty much ran circles around our aircraft, missiles and laser beams.

What is intriguing is that humans reject the obvious fact; if Extraterrestrials intentions were to be violent to us humans I believe they would have already preformed violent acts against us.

Humans have threatened Extraterrestrials with the guns and missiles on aircraft and even with laser beams.

So, "who" is really violent?

I mentioned earlier that Angels "Celestial Entities" were able to travel in space without any craft and only using their nonphysical bodies. They proved this when they were observed by Soviet Astronauts performing this ability in 1985. The Celestial Entities were observed by the Soviet Astronauts flying in space outside their spacecraft.

Hybrid Celestial Entities "Nephilims" as they are called in the bible have attempted to create colonies on earth with the help of the Anakites in different areas on this planet and they finally settled to living on the moon and at the bottom of the ocean, where they could not be observed.

I believe recently some form of life in what appeared to be a small city size colony was detected off the coast of Los Angeles. The small city size colony was at the bottom of the ocean off the coast of Los Angeles, I wonder how long it has been there, maybe since before 1945! That was when the Army was shooting at a craft in the Los Angeles sky.

The craft Extraterrestrials are using now are capable of maintaining a way of life that is comfortable and safe.

Pilots and passengers traveling in airplanes have observed huge cigar shaped craft, some of these craft are supposed to be bigger than our present day nuclear aircraft carrier and they are also equivalent in purpose – a self-contained city.

These Extraterrestrials "Nephilim" craft can travel at amazing speeds, regardless of their size and it can become invisible.

These huge craft are not built specifically for combat as our aircraft carrier, but they are capable of defending themselves.

Smaller craft travel to and from the huge cigar shaped craft.

Some of these huge craft are also circular and V shaped.

These huge shaped craft have been at the bottom of the ocean for thousands of years and they served as habitats for the Nephilims that have remained on earth or on the moon.

Five shapes of Extraterrestrial craft.

Small Quick Craft

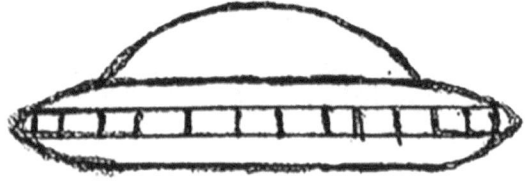

Larger about 100 feet in length

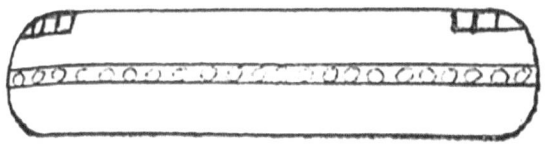

Large cigar shaped craft about 1000 to 3000 feet

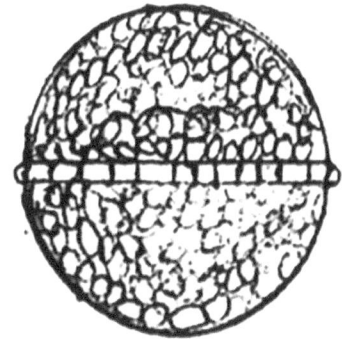

Round shaped about 3000 feet in diameter

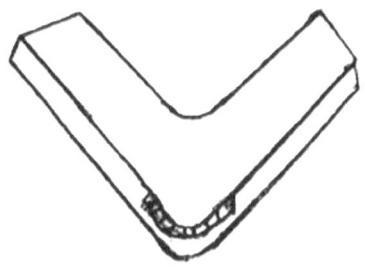

V shaped about 3000 feet tip to tip

Some humans in their make believe fantasies' even want to give the Extraterrestrials credit for populating the earth, even though Extraterrestrials have only existed less than twenty thousand years.

Neanderthal humanoids have existed over one hundred fifty thousand years. The first Cro-Magnon humans have existed over fifty thousand years. The second Cro-Magnon humans have existed over twenty thousand years. How could Nephilims "Extraterrestrials" be responsible for populating the earth?

Yet, you could say Aliens have populated the earth. Aliens are Angels and they and earth woman produced – the Nephilims – that were born on earth.

Maybe, Nephilims "Extraterrestrials" live thousands of years. I am certain that their mother's lives were limited to the same time limits of humans at that time.

I believe Celestial Entities "Angels" live forever. That means they would be privy to the creation of the universe.

We humans don't know very much about Celestial Entities "Angels". Some humans don't even believe Angels are real.

Yet the same individual that made the statement about Angels not being real also made the statement "Anakites means – they who from the heavens came". Since Anakites are Angel in their physical bodies, I would say Angels exist.

Humans and half-humans tend to test the boundaries of evil. I believe evil is what has caused humans all the misery and wars on earth.

Nephilims also have had misery and wars – as documented in the India text the Mahabharata.

The wars described in those writings I believe were real and actually happened in those time periods.

I believe the stories told in the Mahabharata writings by the people of India accurately describe the fact that there were craft which they called "Vimanas" and that there were air battles that happened at the time of the writings.

I believe that is why Mohengo-dira has increases levels of radiation and vitrification is evident there.

I believe that Nephilims were probably trying to prove the old adage that individuals of a certain color are better than any other color.

People that are considered to be white have always considered themselves superior to other shades of color.

I believe that if we examine the history of intelligent individuals, we will be surprised with the outcome.

An example of intelligent individuals, Washington Carver, Albert Einstein, Benjamin Franklin, just to name a few that most people will probably recognize and also realize their skin color.

It is only logical to believe that Nephilims being half-human would resort to deadly conflict to settle a dispute.

The weapons described in the Mahabharata writings would be possible for Nephilims to be using against each other.

These wars were not allowed to continue through the intervention of the Celestial Entities "the fathers" of the Nephilims.

The Celestial Entities "the fathers" had to settle and put an end to the dispute that was getting out of control.

I also believe that the Sirius constellation which is eight light years away from earth is where one group of the Nephilims that were responsible for the conflicts and wars in the east were sent or chose to reside.

That is also why Nephilims on earth make sure a lot of locations on earth point to the larger Orion constellation that is 1500 light years from earth and Orion's belt points to the smaller Sirius constellation.

The statement if Aliens come from the Orion constellation: then maybe we humans also originated there and we came from the Orion constellation.

Again if we want to fantasize, that would only be a fantasy, realistically why would Aliens "Angels" want to bring any one 1500 light years to earth, when the place in the Orion constellation is probably a better place to live.

Angels traveling in their non-physical bodies – the distance 1500 light years – is probably not very difficult.

Someone traveling 1500 light years in a physical body the challenge would be a lot more difficult / impossible.

I heard someone make the statement that they believe that Aliens came to earth in search of gold. Again, you could say that statement is true, but the gold the Aliens "Angels" were looking for was the "gold" in the color of blonde hair.

An Alien "Angel" stating that he comes from the Orion Constellation, that statement is believable and could be true – maybe – heaven is located 1500 light years from earth.

Moving on to another topic, I believe that secrecy is important and I also believe the U.S. Government should be allowed to keep certain secrets. Americans on the other hand should trust and believe honest Americans and other individuals that are only describing what they have seen and/or experienced.

I believe that the individuals in the U.S. Government that knew about the 1947 UFO crash and have knowledge of the recovered "Extraterrestrials" bodies have exposed the truth.

Americans don't want to believe them. I think a lot of people would rather play ignorant than having to deal with the American Government.

Some people would risk everything to tell their stories.

CHAPTER 7

UNIDENTIFIED FLYING OBJECTS "UFOS"

It has been said that Angels are the protectors of the skies.

Humans call Extraterrestrial craft – UFO's – but are they really Unidentified Flying Objects.

I believe humans are intelligent and can distinguish the difference between a craft that is produced and used by humans and a craft that is produced and used by entities with a much higher intelligence.

The higher intelligence demonstrated by Extraterrestrials or as they should be called Nephilims.

The descriptions of verifiable Unidentified Flying Object's are very well described.

Even though the United States government will not admit that such craft are flying in our skies, other countries have come forward and admitted that such craft are flying in their skies.

Very reputable individuals from the United States and different countries have come forward and substantiated numerous sightings in the U.S. and around the world.

I believe the U.S. Government has been secretly reverse engineering certain projects since 1947.

The U.S. Government is probably also communicating with Extraterrestrials but I believe that as in the case of the Nazi's, the Extraterrestrials will only provide a limited amount of technical knowledge.

I believe it is time to move on and quit trying to have the U.S. Government reveal what they know.

The U.S. Government will not admit that they are not telling the truth about UFO's or Extraterrestrials.

Some countries are treating the subject of Extraterrestrial and UFO's in a serious manner.

Animal Mutilations

Why are they happening?

I mentioned earlier in the book that I believe Nephilims are trying to replace the Nephilims that have been killed in accidents or UFO crashes.

The Nephilims are attempting to duplicate the process of creating milk without maintaining or housing the cow.

They removed, studied and analyzed how the different parts of the cow or horse (female of course) can turn grass into milk. That is why usually only certain parts or organs of the cow or horse are removed.

The surgical precision and the lack of blood at the mutilation site should have provided us with a clue that the Animal Mutilations were being performed by entities utilizing an advance technique and advance instruments.

The procedures performed were not possible or probable to be performed by humans.

Why did Nephilims need milk?

The urgent need for milk, was realized, when the Nephilims started to produce human embryos in their attempt to replace the Nephilims that had died.

The Nephilims needed the milk for the new infants and small children they were producing. Milk provides the minerals and nutrients infants and small children need.

The Nephilims were able to produce and provide the suitable environment that was needed for the embryo to develop and grow.

After the infant was separated from that environment, the infant required a mother's milk and since the embryo was developed without a mother, the Nephilims could not provide the milk needed by the infants.

Women that have been abducted have stated; "that they have experienced their embryos removed".

Some have also stated; "that later they were taken aboard a UFO and saw a child that they could recognize as their own".

Since Nephilims "Extraterrestrials" could not have cows in their spaceships, they required a process that would produce milk without the cow.

This is an example of the arrogance of how humans or half-humans attempt to reproduce a process God conceived.

Humans and half-humans believe they can reproduce a process that God conceived and be able to produce the same results.

I will discuss other examples later in the book.

Humans want to believe they are the highest species of creation but we are not.

Humans on the other hand are special. God provided for every possible human need, both physical and intellectual.

The earth provides us with all our human needs and the protection from almost all the unknown threats.

The moon does more than just protect us from meteors.

The universe provides humans with amazing intellectual challenges and knowledge. If we could understand, then we could use this knowledge for a better world.

Humans are presented with evidence of God the Fathers creation plan and other information in the stars.

Humans manipulate, reject, doubt and want to prove through science that God is not responsible for all creation.

I suggest that we use logic and common sense when evaluating evidence presented to us.

One example, when Angels using their physical bodies procreated with beautiful human woman. The Hybrid Celestial children were born and they and their mothers were cared for by the Angels "fathers of the children" and communities were formed. This is logical and common sense would suggest that this is what happened.

Most humans have trouble accepting information presented in the bible, because they are determined to prove that the bible is NOT presenting the truth, and to them "only" a scientific explanation would be considered and accepted as the truth.

When humans landed on the moon in 1969 the statement was made "this is a giant leap for mankind" and it was.

Humans became Extraterrestrials but that giant leap had been accomplished before.

The Hybrid Celestial community had relocated from earth to the dark side of the moon about eighteen thousand years ago and some are still there.

Some observations have been made and recorded of activity and some very suspicious and unexplainable light flashes have been observed on the dark side of the moon.

Humans want to take credit for knowledge and technology that has been developed over the centuries.

The truth is that the Hybrid Celestial entities "Nephilims" have exposed humans to this knowledge at different times in our history.

The Nephilim communities have increased in numbers from the thousands to the hundred of thousands and that explains why we are seeing more of what we consider Extraterrestrial craft throughout the world.

I believe the Nephilim communities have decided that it is time to let the human population know and present the fact that they are present on earth and they have been sharing the earth and the moon with us for thousands of years.

The Nephilim community has knowledge and technology they would like to share with us, but they want to be cautious with the knowledge they share.

Humans are always interested in any form of advance technology and they have demonstrated that any technology that can be used for warfare is used in that capacity. Humans can look back into history and they will observe that every new technology has always been used for warfare.

Humans are so eager to discover any form of life on other planets, yet humans will not even consider the possibility that an advance life form is residing on this planet.

The evidence is and has been demonstrated throughout the thousands of years, yet we choose to play obtuse (that cannot be possible – what could that be – I really have no idea) and ignore or deny it.

Humans have been listening for any form of transmissions from space and yet we are not capable of receiving any of the transmissions of communications between Nephilims craft that are residing in our oceans or flying in our skies.

Nephilims communicate telepathically; this has been verified and testified to by individuals that have had contact with Extraterrestrials.

Celestial Entities "Angels" don't produce a transmission trial that we humans can trace. That is why we will not be able to trace any form of signals being transmitted.

Of course if you communicate telepathically, you don't require ears and the "grays" extraterrestrials I believe are described as not having ears.

Later I'll get more into describing other "grays" difference and why I think the differences have occurred.

I have discussed some thoughts and question others and I have pondered.

Now I will discuss and try to apply logic to other questions individuals have asked.

Humans have wondered why Nephilims "Extraterrestrials" never leave any tools or evidence behind when they depart from any place they have been or occupied.

An analogy in a certain respect is.

During World War II, Americans located an Island that would serve a certain purpose. We flew there and occupied that Island in the pacific. We flew to that Island and to the people of that Island we probably appeared to fly there from somewhere in the sky.

They probably considered us as "extraterrestrials" coming from another planet or gods with amazing machines that came down from the sky.

They would never have considered that we flew there from another part of the same planet they lived on. Our appearance was similar to them, yet we were a different color, taller and spoke a different language. Our clothing was also different and our flying machines were amazing.

I believe that if we had told them we were gods, they would have believed us.

We had technology they had never seen and we flew there with our amazing machines from the heavens / sky.

When the war ended, we packed everything and left. The people of the Island probably thought we had gone back to the planet we had come from.

We didn't leave anything behind – probably – thinking the people of that Island wouldn't know how to use anything we left or they would have no need for any of the tools if we left some behind.

In antiquity Nephilims and their fathers (Angels) played the roles of gods for us humans and amazed us with their superior knowledge and technology.

Humans are discovering structures that are making us realize that history does not follow the path that we humans created and have told over the centuries.

Humans that read the Holy Bible are probably aware that humans were building structures, over fifteen thousand years ago.

The Tower of Babel was built after the flood.

The bible states: Gen 11: 1-7

Then the whole world had one language and a common speech. As men moved eastward they found a plain in Shinar and settled there.

They said to each other, "Come, let's make brick and bake them thoroughly." They used brick instead of stone, and tar for mortar. Then they said, "Come let us build ourselves a city, with a tower that reaches the heavens, so that we may make a name for ourselves and not be scattered over the face of the whole earth.

But the Lord came down to see the city and the tower that the men were building. The Lord said, "If as one people speaking the same language they have begun to do this, then nothing they plan to do will be impossible for them.

Come, let us go down and confuse their language so they will not understand each other."

Humans are not as smart as they think they are, because God can know our thoughts and then God can perform acts that will keep us humans from doing things we should not do.

CHAPTER 8

SOME AFTER THOUGHTS TO TOPICS DISCUSSED EARLIER.

One unique Egyptian pharaoh attempted to convince the Egyptian people that he was a descendent of the gods.

That there is only one God was presented by Akhenaton. Humans rejected the idea then and some reject the idea now.

I believe the Egyptian pharaoh Akhenaton was a Nephilim who was trying to enlighten us humans and share Celestial knowledge which he had acquired from Celestial Entities, who were called gods, making him a descendent of the gods.

Some humans are now trying to give credit to extraterrestrials, evolution and any other means they can conceive for the presence/creation of humans.

Many humans tend to reject any presentation of Celestial knowledge, and skeptics have a propensity to ridicule anything they don't agree with. There are men determined to foolishly discredit any information presented.

I believe that Nephilims technical knowledge helped in the building of the pyramids in Egypt and other locations on earth.

Most of the pyramids on earth and in Egypt are set in a configuration so that they are aligned to track the Orion and Sirius constellations. Orion's belt points to the Sirius constellation that is about 8 light years from earth.

The Mayans learned their astronomical knowledge and to track the Orion and Sirius constellations from the Celestial Entities "Angels" not the Nephilims.

I believe the Nephilims are attempting to direct our attention to these two constellations.

The purpose must be very important to all Nephilims and they don't want us humans to have that attention destroyed or forgotten.

It is interesting hearing a statement "there is one point in space where knowledge comes from". I believe that point would be "Heaven" because that is where the Angels reside.

Nephilims using the advance knowledge and help of their fathers "Angels" have developed their craft to the highest level of technology.

I believe Nephilims are trying to get our attention and would like for us humans to acknowledge them.

That is why they fly their huge craft as close to our aircraft as they do without causing us any harm or interfering with the operation of the aircraft.

I believe the Nephilims are trying to communicate with us humans to share their technology and create a better world.

I believe that the 2000 year old paintings with what appear to be flying craft only represent Nephilims verifying what was written in the bible. It is not surprising to see them in 2000-year-old paintings.

I believe they were also seen flying in the skies during the middle ages.

Nephilims have been on earth less than twenty thousand years. They have been flying in what we call UFO's almost eighteen thousand years.

I spoke earlier of the Neanderthal humanoid both male and female. The Neanderthal man and woman were created and placed on earth by God. The Neanderthal humanoid is rugged, large, physically fit and a survivor that I believe still roams the earth.

Neanderthal humanoids have large human like bodies that are covered with hair and with facial features that almost resemble humans, but are still ape like in appearance.

Neanderthal humanoids are not able to communicate verbally.

Their intelligence is enough to allow them to survive but not progress above the hunter gather stage.

Neanderthal humanoids have increased in numbers and that is why humans are seeing them in more places.

Neanderthal women are not beautiful and they were not appealing to the sons of God "Angels" so they chose not to procreate with the Neanderthal women.

Then came Gods first creation of man "in his image and likeness" – Cro-Magnon humans.

The Cro-Magnon humans were created hairless and thus they had to be covered with animal skins for warmth.

The Cro-Magnon women were better looking than the Neanderthal women but they had brown hair, brown eyes and brown skin and again the sons of God "Angels" chose not to procreate with them.

God's final creation of Cro-Magnon man "in his image and likeness" was Adam and Eve.

The bible states; Gen. 6: 1-3 "When man began to increase in number on the earth and daughters were born to them, the sons of God saw that the daughters of men were beautiful, and they married any of them they chose"

I believe the sons of God "Angels" saw the white skin, blonde hair and blue eyes woman and that is when they considered the daughters of men beautiful.

The sons of God "Angels" only saw the beautiful woman and did not consider the children that would be born.

The Angels "the sons of God" either did not understand or were not aware that the children born from these beautiful woman would not only produce white skinned, blonde hair and blue eyed children but that brown skinned, brown hair and brown eyed children would also be produced.

Nephilims have been observed by individuals that have been taken into the UFO craft and they have said they saw Nephilims "Extraterrestrials" possessing white skin, being over six feet tall with blonde hair and blue eyes.

I believe these are the newest additions to the Nephilims population because they had ears, noses and mouths.

Individual have stated that maybe Extraterrestrials are trying to integrate into the human race.

I don't believe that is their intension, I believe that they look more human because they are using human eggs acquired from women that have been abducted.

Nephilims maybe live thousands of years and that is why they had to produce a covering for their bodies, to protect them from the suns radiation.

Extraterrestrials described as "Grays" because of the color of their supposed skin. I believe the Gray color of their skin is due to an artificial covering for their bodies and wraparound sunglasses with the potential of night vision and normal vision with protection for their eyes.

Nephilims are still capable of dying as it was demonstrated when they crashed in Texas and New Mexico.

I believe Nephilims are not allowed to reside on the planet earth but they can reside in their spaceships at the bottom of the ocean or in the permanent facilities on the moon.

Maybe this was the cause of the conflict described in the Mahabharata writings by the people of India.

We may never know the reason unless the Nephilims are willing to share that part of their history with us humans.

There are individuals that make statements such as there is no such thing as Angels or God did not cause certain events to happen. The individual said "Angels" are only flesh and blood Extraterrestrials and Extraterrestrials are probably responsible for humans being on earth.

A lot of events describe in the bible such as the burning bush that doesn't burn or the pillar of fire that led the Israelites during the night and the cloud that led them during the day.

Nephilims "Extraterrestrials" would have no reason for attempting these events. God could produce these events only by saying for them to happen.

The parting of the Red sea and the Israelites crossing on DRY ground, all these events are accredited to science or Extraterrestrials. Individuals that believe or are making these statements are fantasizing about Extraterrestrials or the other fantasies they express like Extraterrestrials traveling here from another planet or galaxy.

If you don't believe in God, then just say so. The statement

That God could not or would not cause certain events is as ridiculous as saying Angels don't exist only because you have never seen one. God's power and ability are limitless.

Skeptics asked, if the Egyptians had the electric light bulb – where are the wires? I suggest that logic dictates that the wires used by the Egyptians were probably made of gold.

Gold strips were used since the light bulbs were used in the service of the pharaoh. When the light bulbs were not used any more, they were removed by the Extraterrestrials. The batteries were discarded and were found and the gold wire strips were melted and reused for jewelry.

An artifact found in Saqqara Egypt, that was called the Saqqara bird, I believe was left by the Extraterrestrials as an example of the type of aircraft we humans would be capable of producing and flying with our technology.

The Saqqara bird was duplicated, enlarged and tested. It was so aerodynamically sound that it flew and landed properly to everyone's amazement.

Anakites are mentioned in the bible Deuteronomy 1: 28

The word Anakites is supposed to mean "those who from the haven came to earth". Then Anakites means "Angels" because Angels are Celestial Entities and they come from haven.

In Deuteronomy 1: 28 it states; the Anakites were feared because the people they associated with were stronger and taller and their cities were large, with walls up to the sky.

Anakites are what Celestial Entities "Angels" are called when they are using their physical bodies on earth.

Why would the people in those cities build walls to the sky if it wasn't to keep other people from seeing inside?

I believe Nephilims built the cities, which were probably, more advance than anything the people living outside the cities could imagine.

I have heard the question asked – where did the people – that built the pyramids or any of the structures that require advance knowledge to build, get the knowledge.

The book of Enoch tell us how the Angels were instructed by God to teach Enoch a lot of advance knowledge.

That demonstrates how much advance knowledge Angels are entrusted with and what they are capable of using.

Why are we surprised to find pyramids built all over the earth?

Humans attempted to build a tower to reach the heavens and they were stopped by God – the tower of Babel Gen. 11:1

The reason the tower of Babel is called Babel is because at the tower of Babel is where the Lord confused the language of the whole world. Gen. 11: 9

Pyramids are the means that Nephilims use to let us humans know that an advance technology is used to erect these structures.

We talk about giants as if they are a myth and they never existed. We have giants on earth now.

They are called basketball players, well not all of them are basketball players.

Most people will probable laugh at the last sentence.

What is a giant?

I would call any person that is taller than seven feet a giant. The tallest man on record is more than eight feet tall.

The average man is about 6 foot and the average woman is about 5 feet 8 inches.

When big foot is recognized as the humanoid that they are, we will also call them giants.

What I don't understand is that if the Russians shot a creature that appeared to resemble what is called Big Foot.

Why are scientist not presenting the findings – is this a government cover up. It amazes me what ridiculous explanations scientist and other people are making or are asked to make to explain unexplainable events.

I believe the Greeks were taught by Apollo, whom they called a god. Apollo was NOT a god, if anything Apollo was a Celestial Entity and they are not gods.

Another interesting point is that Apollo taught the Greeks to build and Astronomy, subjects the Celestial Entities were well versed about.

Earlier, I mentioned that Extraterrestrials or Celestial Entities had exposed humans to advance knowledge via a direct exposure.

The Greeks presented the proof in a make believe story.

This is how the evidence was presented to us humans in antiquity and we have no problem believing because it is in a story form with imaginary characters.

This was the only form of expressing or the use for an explanation for what was happening at the time.

We humans accept stories expressed or explained in this fashion, yet we doubt and/or ridicule any person that tries to present an event that they have observed.

Humans are afraid of Extraterrestrials because we are afraid of the unknown.

Yet, humans will allow themselves to create imaginary scary and grotesque looking entities and portray them as Extraterrestrials.

The appearance of Extraterrestrials that humans have knowledge of is that they are 4 to 5 feet tall with thin wiry bodies, big heads and dark slanted eyes.

Humans could probably accept Extraterrestrials as described above, not as ordinary looking, but at least not scary or grotesque.

Then if Extraterrestrials appearance is not what humans would consider scary, maybe what humans are really scared about is the technology of the Extraterrestrials.

Humans are afraid that the Extraterrestrials will perform – what we would call experiments – on humans.

Extraterrestrials are known for performing probing procedures and taking samples.

That would be scary, I know many people that are scared of going to a clinic or the hospital where the doctor explains a procedure he intend to perform, and that is scary. Now take a complete stranger that doesn't explain anything and starts performing procedures on you – that would petrify anyone.

Especially if the stranger that doesn't even look human and he is performing these procedures on you. Then add to that, images of scary and grotesque entities – no wonder we are scared of Extraterrestrials.

My theory is:

Nephilims "Extraterrestrials" have lived for thousands of years and they are very old. Maybe their bodies are aging and just like us humans "they" want to live longer. They are attempting to prolong their lives by the use of their technology.

They are attempting to use samples from humans but I don't believe the samples are compatible.

I saw a program where an individual attempted to extract the face of Jesus Christ from the cloth of Turin which was used to cover Jesus Christ at the time of his death.

It was interesting how various reasons were given in producing the proposed image of the face of Jesus Christ.

I wonder what the results would be if an opinion poll was taken of the likeness of the final outcome for the face of Jesus Christ and the image shown on the cloth of Turin.

I also wonder how much demographics and preconceptions affected the outcome.

I believe the Jews in the time of Jesus Christ also had a difficulty accepting Jesus Christ because of his appearance.

Jesus Christ image on the cloth of Turin is there so that we humans would have no doubt of his appearance.

If we believe in Jesus Christ – then we believe in God. Humans should quit trying to circumvent or manipulate Gods words – because if they are wrong in their attempts and God is real – they will have to answer for their indiscretions.

My final thought is about Celestial Entities "Angels - Aliens". Celestial Entities were created by God – let us say – before earth was created.

That would be over 4 and a half billion years ago. Now, here they are wondering the universe – again let us say – they travel at the speed of light in their nonphysical bodies and the universe is billions of light years across.

Their wondering and checking different galaxies would take them billions of years or more to explore in one direction.

More than sixty five million years ago while wondering they discover that God had populated earth with creatures. They came to earth and since they have the ability of possessing physical or nonphysical bodies they choose to use their physical bodies and walk around with the dinosaurs.

I believe someone discovered what looks like a human feet print next to a dinosaur feet print and dinosaurs went extinct sixty five million years ago, that could explain the feet print.

I don't believe humans are capable of comprehending the abilities of Celestial Entities. Their position in the hierarchy

of Celestial Entities, I believe also describes their appearance.

This means that Celestial Entities have different appearance.

We will probably never know the different appearance, but I believe that the closer the Celestial Entities are to the presence of God the taller and larger they are.

I have heard individuals say that Aliens have probably been around millions of years and that is why they have the superior technology. Celestial Entities – Angels or Aliens as we call them have been around billions of years.

Celestial Entities – Angels – Aliens – they are all the same Entity's, never needed any type of craft to travel. The only reason they travel in spacecraft in a physical body is to provide assistance to their Hybrid children the Nephilims or as we call them - Extraterrestrials.

Celestial Entities – the fathers of the Hybrid children – have their hands full in caring and managing the affair of Nephilims.

I hope that the issues presented in this book, everyone is willing to ponder and feel good with the conclusion they reach.

I present the following quote from the Holy Bible NIV;

2 Timothy 3: 14 – 4: 4

"But as for you, continue in what you have learned and have become convinced of, because you know those from whom you have learned it, and how from infancy you have known the holy Scriptures, which are able to make you wise for salvation through faith in Christ Jesus. All Scripture is God-breathed and is useful for teaching, rebuking, correcting and training in righteousness, so that the man of God may be thoroughly equipped for every good work.

In the presence of God and of Christ Jesus, who will judge the living and the dead, and in view of his appearing and his kingdom, I give you this charge: Preach the word; be prepared in season and out of season; correct, rebuke and encourage – with great patience and careful instruction. For the time will come when men will not put up with sound doctrine. Instead, to suit their own desires, they will gather around them a great number of teachers to say what their itching ears want to hear. They will turn their ears away from the truth and turn aside to myth."

www.ingramcontent.com/pod-product-compliance
Lightning Source LLC
LaVergne TN
LVHW090036080526
838202LV00046B/3837